THE

BATTLE OF DORKING

REMINISCENCES OF A VOLUNTEER

FROM

𝔅lackwood's 𝔐agazine

MAY 1871

The Naval & Military Press Ltd

Published by

The Naval & Military Press Ltd

Unit 5 Riverside, Brambleside
Bellbrook Industrial Estate
Uckfield, East Sussex
TN22 1QQ England

Tel: +44 (0)1825 749494

www.naval-military-press.com
www.nmarchive.com

THE BATTLE OF DORKING.

You ask me to tell you, my grandchildren, something about my own share in the great events that happened fifty years ago. 'Tis sad work turning back to that bitter page in our history, but you may perhaps take profit in your new homes from the lesson it teaches. For us in England it came too late. And yet we had plenty of warnings, if we had only made use of them. The danger did not come on us unawares. It burst on us suddenly, 'tis true; but its coming was foreshadowed plainly enough to open our eyes, if we had not been wilfully blind. We English have only ourselves to blame for the humiliation which has been brought on the land. Venerable old age! Dishonourable old age, I say, when it follows a manhood dishonoured as ours has been. I declare, even now, though fifty years have passed, I can hardly look a young man in the face when I think I am one of those in whose youth happened this degradation of Old England—one of those who betrayed the trust handed down to us unstained by our forefathers.

What a proud and happy country was this fifty years ago! Free-trade had been working for more than a quarter of a century, and there seemed to be no end to the riches it was bringing us. London was growing bigger and bigger; you could not build houses fast enough for the rich people who wanted to live in them,

the merchants who made the money and came from all
parts of the world to settle there, and the lawyers and
doctors and engineers and others, and trades-people who
got their share out of the profits. The streets reached
down to Croydon and Wimbledon, which my father
could remember quite country places; and people used
to say that Kingston and Reigate would soon be joined
to London. We thought we could go on building and
multiplying for ever. 'Tis true that even then there was
no lack of poverty; the people who had no money went
on increasing as fast as the rich, and pauperism was
already beginning to be a difficulty; but if the rates were
high, there was plenty of money to pay them with; and
as for what were called the middle classes, there really
seemed no limit to their increase and prosperity. People
in those days thought it quite a matter of course to bring
a dozen of children into the world—or, as it used to be
said, Providence sent them that number of babies; and
if they couldn't always marry off all the daughters, they
used to manage to provide for the sons, for there were
new openings to be found in all the professions, or in the
Government offices, which went on steadily getting
larger. Besides, in those days young men could be sent
out to India, or into the army or navy; and even then
emigration was not uncommon, although not the regular
custom it is now. Schoolmasters, like all other professional classes, drove a capital trade. They did not teach
very much, to be sure, but new schools with their four or
five hundred boys were springing up all over the country.

Fools that we were! We thought that all this wealth
and prosperity were sent us by Providence, and could
not stop coming. In our blindness we did not see that
we were merely a big workshop, making up the things
which came from all parts of the world; and that if other
nations stopped sending us raw goods to work up, we

could not produce them ourselves. True, we had in those days an advantage in our cheap coal and iron; and had we taken care not to waste the fuel, it might have lasted us longer. But even then there were signs that coal and iron would soon become cheaper in foreign parts; while as to food and other things, England was not better off than it is now. We were so rich simply because other nations from all parts of the world were in the habit of sending their goods to us to be sold or manufactured; and we thought that this would last for ever. And so, perhaps, it might have lasted, if we had only taken proper means to keep it; but, in our folly, we were too careless even to insure our prosperity, and after the course of trade was turned away it would not come back again.

And yet, if ever a nation had a plain warning, we had. If we were the greatest trading country, our neighbours were the leading military power in Europe. They were driving a good trade, too, for this was before their foolish communism (about which you will hear when you are older) had ruined the rich without benefiting the poor, and they were in many respects the first nation in Europe; but it was on their army that they prided themselves most. And with reason. They had beaten the Russians and the Austrians, and the Prussians too, in bygone years, and they thought they were invincible. Well do I remember the great review held at Paris by the Emperor Napoleon during the great Exhibition, and how proud he looked showing off his splendid Guards to the assembled kings and princes. Yet, three years afterwards, the force so long deemed the first in Europe was ignominiously beaten, and the whole army taken prisoners. Such a defeat had never happened before in the world's history; and with this proof before us of the folly of disbelieving in the possibility of disaster merely because it had never fallen upon us, it might have been supposed that we should have the sense to take the lesson to heart. And the country was certainly roused for a time, and a cry was raised that the army ought to be reorganised, and our defences strengthened against the enormous power for sudden attacks which it was seen other nations were able to put forth. And a scheme of army reform was brought forward by the Government. It was a half-and-half affair at best; and, unfortunately, instead of being taken up in Parliament as a national scheme, it was made a party matter of, and so fell through. There was a Radical section of the House, too, whose votes had to be secured by conciliation, and which blindly demanded a reduction of armaments as the price of allegiance. This party always decried military establishments as part of a fixed policy for reducing the influence of the Crown and the aristocracy. They could not understand that the times had altogether changed, that the Crown had really no power, and that the Government merely existed at the pleasure of the House of Commons, and that even Parliament-rule was beginning to give way to mob-law. At any rate, the Ministry, baffled on all sides, gave up by degrees all the strong points of a scheme which they were not heartily in earnest about. It was not that there was any lack of money, if only it had been spent in the right way. The army cost enough, and more than enough, to give us a proper defence, and there were armed men of sorts in plenty and to spare, if only they had been decently organised. It was in organisation and forethought that we fell short, because our rulers did not heartily believe in the need for preparation. The fleet and the Channel, they said, were sufficient protection. So army reform was put off to some more convenient season, and the militia and volunteers were left untrained as before, because to call them out for drill would " interfere with the industry of the country." We could

have given up some of the industry of those days, for-
sooth, and yet be busier than we are now. But why
tell you a tale you have so often heard already? The
nation, although uneasy, was misled by the false security
its leaders professed to feel; the warning given by the
disasters that overtook France was allowed to pass by
unheeded. We would not even be at the trouble of
putting our arsenals in a safe place, or of guarding the
capital against a surprise, although the cost of doing so
would not have been so much as missed from the
national wealth. The French trusted in their army and
its great reputation, we in our fleet; and in each case the
result of this blind confidence was disaster, such as our
forefathers in their hardest struggles could not have even
imagined.

I need hardly tell you how the crash came about.
First, the rising in India drew away a part of our small
army; then came the difficulty with America, which had
been threatening for years, and we sent off ten thousand
men to defend Canada—a handful which did not go far
to strengthen the real defences of that country, but formed
an irresistible temptation to the Americans to try and
take them prisoners, especially as the contingent included
three battalions of the Guards. Thus the regular army
at home was even smaller than usual, and nearly half of
it was in Ireland to check the talked-of Fenian invasion
fitting out in the West. Worse still—though I do not
know it would really have mattered as things turned out
—the fleet was scattered abroad: some ships to guard
the West Indies, others to check privateering in the
China seas, and a large part to try and protect our colonies on the Northern Pacific shore of America, where,
with incredible folly, we continued to retain possessions
which we could not possibly defend. America was not
the great power forty years ago that it is now; but for

us to try and hold territory on her shores which could only be reached by sailing round the Horn, was as absurd as if she had attempted to take the Isle of Man before the independence of Ireland. We see this plainly enough now, but we were all blind then.

It was while we were in this state, with our ships all over the world, and our little bit of an army cut up into detachments, that the Secret Treaty was published, and Holland and Denmark were annexed. People say now that we might have escaped the troubles which came on us if we had at any rate kept quiet till our other difficulties were settled ; but the English were always an impulsive lot : the whole country was boiling over with indignation, and the Government, egged on by the press, and going with the stream, declared war. We had always got out of scrapes before, and we believed our old luck and pluck would somehow pull us through.

Then, of course, there was bustle and hurry all over the land. Not that the calling up of the army reserves caused much stir, for I think there were only about 5000 altogether, and a good many of these were not to be found when the time came ; but recruiting was going on all over the country, with a tremendous high bounty, 50,000 more men having been voted for the army. Then there was a Ballot Bill passed for adding 55,500 men to the militia ; why a round number was not fixed on I don't know, but the Prime Minister said that this was the exact quota wanted to put the defences of the country on a sound footing. Then the shipbuilding that began ! Ironclads, despatch-boats, gunboats, monitors,— every building-yard in the country got its job, and they were offering ten shillings a-day wages for anybody who could drive a rivet. This didn't improve the recruiting, you may suppose. I remember, too, there was a squabble in the House of Commons about whether artisans should be drawn for the ballot, as they were so much wanted, and I think they got an exemption. This sent numbers to the yards ; and if we had had a couple of years to prepare instead of a couple of weeks, I daresay we should have done very well.

It was on a Monday that the declaration of war was announced, and in a few hours we got our first inkling of the sort of preparation the enemy had made for the event which they had really brought about, although the actual declaration was made by us. A pious appeal to the God of battles, whom it was said we had aroused, was telegraphed back ; and from that moment all communication with the north of Europe was cut off. Our em bassies and legations were packed off at an hour's notice, and it was as if we had suddenly come back to the middle ages. The dumb astonishment visible all over London the next morning, when the papers came out void of news, merely hinting at what had happened, was one of the most startling things in this war of surprises. But everything had been arranged beforehand ; nor ought we to have been surprised, for we had seen the same Power, only a few months before, move down half a million of men on a few days' notice, to conquer the greatest military nation in Europe, with no more fuss than our War Office used to make over the transport of a brigade from Aldershot to Brighton,—and this, too, without the allies it had now. What happened now was not a bit more wonderful in reality ; but people of this country could not bring themselves to believe that what had never occurred before to England could ever possibly happen. Like our neighbours, we became wise when it was too late.

Of course the papers were not long in getting news— even the mighty organisation set at work could not shut out a special correspondent ; and in a very few days, although the telegraphs and railways were intercepted right across Europe, the main facts oozed out. An embargo had been laid on all the shipping in every port from the Baltic to Ostend; the fleets of the two great Powers had moved out, and it was supposed were assembled in the great northern harbour, and troops were hurrying on board all the steamers detained in these places, most of which were British vessels. It was clear that invasion was intended. Even then we might have been saved, if the fleet had been ready. The forts which guarded the flotilla were perhaps too strong for shipping to attempt; but an ironclad or two, handled as British sailors knew how to use them, might have destroyed or damaged a part of the transports, and delayed the expedition, giving us what we wanted, time. But then the best part of the fleet had been decoyed down to the Dardanelles, and what remained of the Channel squadron was looking after Fenian filibusters off the west of Ireland; so it was ten days before the fleet was got together, and by that time it was plain the enemy's preparations were too far advanced to be stopped by a *coup-de-main*. Information, which came chiefly through Italy, came slowly, and was more or less vague and uncertain; but this much was known, that at least a couple of hundred thousand men were embarked or ready to be put on board ships, and that the flotilla was guarded by more ironclads than we could then muster. I suppose it was the uncertainty as to the point the enemy would aim at for landing, and the fear lest he should give us the go-by, that kept the fleet for several days in the Downs; but it was not until the Tuesday fortnight after the declaration of war that it weighed anchor and steamed away for the North Sea. Of course you have read about the Queen's visit to the fleet the day before, and how she sailed round the ships in her yacht, and went on board the flag-ship to take leave of the admiral; how, overcome with emotion, she told him that the safety of the country was committed to his keeping. You remember, too, the gallant old officer's reply, and how all the ships' yards were manned, and how lustily the tars cheered as her Majesty was rowed off. The account was of course telegraphed to London, and the high spirits of the fleet infected the whole town. I was outside the Charing Cross station when the Queen's special train from Dover arrived, and from the cheering and shouting which greeted her Majesty as she drove away, you might have supposed we had already won a great victory. The leading journal, which had gone in strongly for the army reduction carried out during the session, and had been nervous and desponding in tone during the past fortnight, suggesting all sorts of compromises as a way of getting out of the war, came out in a very jubilant form next morning. " Panic-stricken inquirers," it said, "ask now, where are the means of meeting the invasion ? We reply that the invasion will never take place. A British fleet, manned by British sailors whose courage and enthusiasm are reflected in the people of this country, is already on the way to meet the presumptuous foe. The issue of a contest between British ships and those of any other country, under anything like equal odds, can never be doubtful. England awaits with calm confidence the issue of the impending action."

Such were the words of the leading article, and so we all felt. It was on Tuesday, the 10th of August, that the fleet sailed from the Downs. It took with it a submarine cable to lay down as it advanced, so that continuous communication was kept up, and the papers were publishing special editions every few minutes with the latest news. This was the first time such a thing had been done, and the feat was accepted as a good omen. Whether it is true that the Admiralty made use of the cable to keep on sending contradictory orders, which took the command out of the admiral's hands, I can't say; but all that the admiral sent in return was a few messages of the briefest kind, which neither the Admiralty nor any one else could have made any use of. Such a ship had gone off reconnoitring; such another had rejoined—fleet was in latitude so and so. This went on till the Thursday morning. I had just come up to town by train as usual, and was walking to my office, when the newsboys began to cry, "New edition—enemy's fleet in sight!" You may imagine the scene in London! Business still went on at the banks, for bills matured although the independence of the country was being fought out under our own eyes, so to say, and the speculators were active enough. But even with the people who were making and losing their fortunes, the interest in the fleet overcame everything else; men who went to pay in or draw out their money stopped to show the last bulletin to the cashier. As for the street, you could hardly get along for the crowd stopping to buy and read the papers; while at every house or office the members sat restlessly in the common room, as if to keep together for company, sending out some one of their number every few minutes to get the latest edition. At least this is what happened at our office; but to sit still was as impossible as to do anything, and most of us went out and wandered about among the crowd, under a sort of feeling that the news was got quicker at in this way. Bad as were the times coming, I think the sickening suspense of that day, and the shock which followed, was almost the worst that we underwent. It was about ten o'clock that the first telegram came; an hour later the wire announced that the admiral had signalled to form line of battle, and shortly afterwards that the order was given to bear down on the enemy and engage. At twelve came the announcement, "Fleet opened fire about three miles to leeward of us"—that is, the ship with the cable. So far all had been expectancy, then came the first token of calamity. "An ironclad has been blown up"—"the enemy's torpedoes are doing great damage"—"the flag-ship is laid aboard the enemy"—"the flag-ship appears to be sinking"—"the vice-admiral has signalled to"—there the cable became silent, and, as you know, we heard no more till, two days afterwards, the solitary ironclad which escaped the disaster steamed into Portsmouth.

Then the whole story came out—how our sailors, gallant as ever, had tried to close with the enemy; how the latter evaded the conflict at close quarters, and, sheering off, left behind them the fatal engines which sent our ships, one after the other, to the bottom; how all this happened almost in a few minutes. The Government, it appears, had received warnings of this invention; but to the nation this stunning blow was utterly unexpected. That Thursday I had to go home early for regimental drill, but it was impossible to remain doing nothing, so when that was over I went up to town again, and after waiting in expectation of news which never came, and missing the midnight train, I walked home. It was a hot sultry night, and I did not arrive till near sunrise. The whole town was quite still—the lull before the storm; and as I let myself in with my latch-key, and went softly up-stairs to my room to avoid waking the sleeping household, I could not but contrast the peacefulness of the morning—no sound breaking the silence but the singing of the birds in the garden—with the passionate remorse and indignation that would break out with the day. Perhaps the inmates of the rooms were as wakeful as myself; but the house in its stillness was just as it used to be when I came home alone from balls or parties in the happy days gone by. Tired though I was, I could not sleep, so I went down to the river and had a swim; and on returning found the household was assembling for early breakfast. A sorrowful household it was, although the burden pressing on each was partly an unseen one. My father, doubting whether his firm could last through the day; my mother, her distress about my brother, now with his regiment on the coast, already exceeding that which she felt for the public misfortune, had come down, although hardly fit to leave her room. My sister Clara was worst of all, for she could not but try to disguise her special interest in the fleet; and though we had all guessed that her heart was given to the young lieutenant in the flag-ship—the first vessel to go down—a love unclaimed could not be told, nor could we express the sympathy we felt for the poor girl. That breakfast, the last meal we ever had together, was soon ended, and my father and I went up to town by an early train, and got there just as the fatal announcement of the loss of the fleet was telegraphed from Portsmouth.

The panic and excitement of that day—how the funds went down to 35; the run upon the bank and its stoppage; the fall of half the houses in the city; how the Government issued a notification suspending specie payment and the tendering of bills—this last precaution too late for most firms, Graham & Co. among the number, which stopped payment as soon as my father got to the office; the call to arms, and the unanimous response of the country—all this is history which I need not repeat. You wish to hear about my own share in the business of the time. Well, volunteering had increased immensely from the day war was proclaimed, and our regiment went up in a day or two from its usual strength of 600 to nearly 1000. But the stock of rifles was deficient. We were promised a further supply in a few days, which however, we never received; and while waiting for them

the regiment had to be divided into two parts, the recruits drilling with the rifles in the morning, and we old
hands in the evening. The failures and stoppage of
work on this black Friday threw an immense number of
young men out of employment, and we recruited up to
1400 strong by the next day; but what was the use of
all these men without arms? On the Saturday it was
announced that a lot of smooth-bore muskets in store at
the Tower would be served out to regiments applying for
them, and a regular scramble took place among the
volunteers for them, and our people got hold of a couple
of hundred. But you might almost as well have tried to
learn rifle-drill with a broom-stick as with old brown bess;
besides, there was no smooth-bore ammunition in the
country. A national subscription was opened for the
manufacture of rifles at Birmingham, which ran up to a
couple of millions in two days, but, like everything else,
this came too late. To return to the volunteers: camps
had been formed a fortnight before at Dover, Brighton,
Harwich, and other places, of regulars and militia, and
the headquarters of most of the volunteer regiments were
attached to one or other of them, and the volunteers
themselves used to go down for drill from day to day, as
they could spare time, and on Friday an order went out
that they should be permanently embodied; but the metropolitan volunteers were still kept about London as a
sort of reserve, till it could be seen at what point the
invasion would take place. We were all told off to
brigades and divisions. Our brigade consisted of the 4th
Royal Surrey Militia, the 1st Surrey Administrative Battalion, as it was called, at Clapham, the 7th Surrey
Volunteers at Southwark, and ourselves; but only our
battalion and the militia were quartered in the same
place, and the whole brigade had merely two or three
afternoons together at brigade exercise in Bushev Park

before the march took place. Our brigadier belonged to a line regiment in Ireland, and did not join till the very morning the order came. Meanwhile, during the preliminary fortnight, the militia colonel commanded. But though we volunteers were busy with our drill and preparations, those of us who, like myself, belonged to Government offices, had more than enough of office work to do, as you may suppose. The volunteer clerks were allowed to leave office at four o'clock, but the rest were kept hard at the desk far into the night. Orders to the lord-lieutenants, to the magistrates, notifications, all the arrangements for cleaning out the workhouses for hospitals—these and a hundred other things had to be managed in our office, and there was as much bustle indoors as out. Fortunate we were to be so busy—the people to·be pitied were those who had nothing to do. And on Sunday (that was the 15th August) work went on just as usual. We had an early parade and drill, and I went up to town by the nine o'clock train in my uniform, taking·my rifle with me in case of accidents, and luckily too, as it turned out, a mackintosh overcoat. When I got to Waterloo there were all sorts of rumours afloat. A fleet had been seen off the Downs, and some of the despatch-boats which were hovering about the coasts brought news that there was a large flotilla off Harwich, but nothing could be seen from the shore, as the weather was hazy. The enemy's light ships had taken and sunk all the fishing-boats they could catch, to prevent the news of their whereabouts reaching us; but a few escaped during the night and reported that the Inconstant frigate coming home from North America, without any knowledge of what had taken place, had sailed right into the enemy's fleet and been captured. In town the troops were all getting ready for a move; the Guards in the Wellington Barracks were under arms, and their baggage·

waggons packed and drawn up in the Bird-cage Walk. The usual guard at the Horse Guards had been withdrawn, and orderlies and staff-officers were going to and fro. All this I saw on the way to my office, where I worked away till twelve o'clock, and then feeling hungry after my early breakfast, I went across Parliament Street to my club to get some luncheon. There were about half-a-dozen men in the coffee-room, none of whom I knew; but in a minute or two Danvers of the Treasury entered in a tremendous hurry. From him I got the first bit of authentic news I had had that day. The enemy had landed in force near Harwich, and the metropolitan regiments were ordered down there to reinforce the troops already collected in that neighbourhood; his regiment was to parade at one o'clock, and he had come to get something to eat before starting. We bolted a hurried lunch, and were just leaving the club when a messenger from the Treasury came running into the hall.

"Oh, Mr Danvers," said he, "I've come to look for you, sir; the secretary says that all the gentlemen are wanted at the office, and that you must please not one of you go with the regiments."

"The devil!" cried Danvers.

"Do you know if that order extends to all the public offices?" I asked.

"I don't know," said the man, "but I believe it do. I know there's messengers gone round to all the clubs and luncheon-bars to look for the gentlemen; the secretary says it's quite impossible any one can be spared just now, there's so much work to do; there's orders just come to send off our records to Birmingham to-night."

I did not wait to condole with Danvers, but, just glancing up Whitehall to see if any of our messengers were in pursuit, I ran off as hard as I could for Westminster Bridge, and so to the Waterloo station.

The place had quite changed its aspect since the morning. The regular service of trains had ceased, and the station and approaches were full of troops, among them the Guards and artillery. Everything was very orderly: the men had piled arms, and were standing about in groups. There was no sign of high spirits or enthusiasm. Matters had become too serious. Every man's face reflected the general feeling that we had neglected the warnings given us, and that now the danger so long derided as impossible and absurd had really come and found us unprepared. But the soldiers, if grave, looked determined, like men who meant to do their duty whatever might happen. A train full of guardsmen was just starting for Guildford. I was told it would stop at Surbiton, and, with several other volunteers, hurrying like myself to join our regiment, got a place in it. We did not arrive a moment too soon, for the regiment was marching from Kingston down to the station. The destination of our brigade was the east coast. Empty carriages were drawn up in the siding, and our regiment was to go first. A large crowd was assembled to see it off, including the recruits who had joined during the last fortnight, and who formed by far the largest part of our strength. They were to stay behind, and were certainly very much in the way already; for as all the officers and sergeants belonged to the active part, there was no one to keep discipline among them, and they came crowding around us, breaking the ranks and making it difficult to get into the train. Here I saw our new brigadier for the first time. He was a soldier-like man, and no doubt knew his duty, but he appeared new to volunteers, and did not seem to know how to deal with gentlemen privates. I wanted very much to run home and get my greatcoat and knapsack, which I had bought a few days ago, but feared to be left behind ; a good-natured recruit volun-

teered to fetch them for me, but he had not returned before we started, and I began the campaign with a kit consisting of a mackintosh and a small pouch of tobacco.

It was a tremendous squeeze in the train; for, besides
the ten men sitting down, there were three or four standing up in every compartment, and the afternoon was
close and sultry, and there were so many stoppages on
the way that we took nearly an hour and a half crawling
up to Waterloo. It was between five and six in the
afternoon when we arrived there, and it was nearly seven
before we marched up to the Shoreditch station. The
whole place was filled up with stores and ammunition,
to be sent off to the east, so we piled arms in the street
and scattered about to get food and drink, of which most
of us stood in need, especially the latter, for some were
already feeling the worse for the heat and crush. I was
just stepping into a public-house with Travers, when who
should drive up but his pretty wife? Most of our friends
had paid their adieus at the Surbiton station, but she
had driven up by the road in his brougham, bringing
their little boy to have a last look at papa. She had also
brought his knapsack and greatcoat, and, what was still
more acceptable, a basket containing fowls, tongue, bread-
and-butter, and biscuits, and a couple of bottles of claret,
—which priceless luxuries they insisted on my sharing.

Meanwhile the hours went on. The 4th Surrey
Militia, which had marched all the way from Kingston,
had come up, as well as the other volunteer corps; the
station had been partly cleared of the stores that encum-
bered it; some artillery, two militia regiments, and a
battalion of the line, had been despatched, and our turn
to start had come, and long lines of carriages were drawn
up ready for us; but still we remained in the street.
You may fancy the scene. There seemed to be as many
people as ever in London, and we could hardly move

for the crowds of spectators—fellows hawking fruits and volunteers' comforts, hewsboys and so forth, to say nothing of the cabs and omnibuses; while orderlies and staff-officers were constantly riding up with messages. A good many of the militiamen, and some of our people too, had taken more than enough to drink; perhaps a hot sun had told on empty stomachs; anyhow, they became very noisy. The din, dirt, and heat were indescribable. So the evening wore on, and all the information our officers could get from the brigadier, who appeared to be acting under another general, was, that orders had come to stand fast for the present. Gradually the street became quieter and cooler. The brigadier, who, by way of setting an example, had remained for some hours without leaving his saddle, had got a chair out of a shop, and sat nodding in it; most of the men were lying down or sitting on the pavement — some sleeping, some smoking. In vain had Travers begged his wife to go home. She declared that, having come so far, she would stay and see the last of us. The brougham had been sent away to a by-street, as it blocked up the road; so he sat on a doorstep, she by him on the knapsack. Little Arthur, who had been delighted at the bustle and the uniforms, and in high spirits, became at last very cross, and eventually cried himself to sleep in his father's arms, his golden hair and one little dimpled arm hanging over his shoulder. Thus went on the weary hours, till suddenly the assembly sounded, and we all started up. We were to return to Waterloo. The landing on the east was only a feint—so ran the rumour—the real attack was on the south. Anything seemed better than indecision and delay, and, tired though we were, the march back was gladly hailed. Mrs Travers, who made us take the remains of the luncheon with us, we left to look for her carriage; little Arthur, who was awake again, but very good and quiet, in her arms.

We did not reach Waterloo till nearly midnight, and there was some delay in starting again. Several volunteer and militia regiments had arrived from the north; the station and all its approaches were jammed up with men, and trains were being despatched away as fast as they could be made up. All this time no news had reached us since the first announcement; but the excitement then aroused had now passed away under the influence of fatigue and want of sleep, and most of us dozed off as soon as we got under way. I did, at any rate, and was awoke by the train stopping at Leatherhead. There was an up-train returning to town, and some persons in it were bringing up news from the coast. We could not, from our part of the train, hear what they said, but the rumour was passed up from one carriage to another. The enemy had landed in force at Worthing. Their position had been attacked by the troops from the camp near Brighton, and the action would be renewed in the morning. The volunteers had behaved very well. This was all the information we could get. So, then, the invasion had come at last. It was clear, at any rate, from what was said, that the enemy had not been driven back yet, and we should be in time most likely to take a share in the defence. It was sunrise when the train crawled into Dorking, for there had been numerous stoppages on the way; and here it was pulled up for a long time, and we were told to get out and stretch ourselves—an order gladly responded to, for we had been very closely packed all night. Most of us, too, took the opportunity to make an early breakfast off the food we had brought from Shoreditch. I had the remains of Mrs Travers's fowl and some bread wrapped up in my waterproof, which I shared with one or two less provident comrades. We

could see from our halting-place that the line was blocked
with trains beyond and behind. It must have been
about eight o'clock when we got orders to take our
seats again, and the train began to move slowly on
towards Horsham. Horsham Junction was the point to
be occupied—so the rumour went; but about ten o'clock,
when halting at a small station a few miles short of it,
the order came to leave the train, and our brigade formed
in column on the highroad. Beyond us was some field-
artillery; and further on, so we were told by a staff-
officer, another brigade, which was to make up a division
with ours. After more delays the line began to move,
but not forwards; our route was towards the north-west,
and a sort of suspicion of the state of affairs flashed
across my mind. Horsham was already occupied by the
enemy's advanced-guard, and we were to fall back on
Leith Common, and take up a position threatening his
flank, should he advance either to Guildford or Dorking.
This was soon confirmed by what the colonel was told
by the brigadier and passed down the ranks; and just
now, for the first time, the boom of artillery came up on
the light south breeze. In about an hour the firing
ceased. What did it mean? We could not tell. Meanwhile our march continued. The day was very close
and sultry, and the clouds of dust stirred up by our feet
almost suffocated us. I had saved a soda-water-bottleful
of yesterday's claret; but this went only a short way, for
there were many mouths to share it with, and the thirst
soon became as bad as ever. Several of the regiment fell
out from faintness, and we made frequent halts to rest
and let the stragglers come up. At last we reached the
top of Leith Hill. It is a striking spot, being the highest
point in the south of England. The view from it is
splendid, and most lovely did the country look this
summer day, although the grass was brown from the long

drought. It was a great relief to get from the dusty road
on to the common, and at the top of the hill there was a
refreshing breeze. We could see now, for the first time,
the whole of our division. Our own regiment did not
muster more than 500, for it contained a large number
of Government office men who had been detained, like
Danvers, for duty in town, and others were not much
larger; but the militia regiment was very strong, and
the whole division, I was told, mustered nearly 5000
rank and file. We could see other troops also in exten-
sion of our division, and could count a couple of field-
batteries of Royal Artillery, besides some heavy guns,
belonging to the volunteers apparently, drawn by cart-
horses. The cooler air, the sense of numbers, and the
evident strength of the position we held, raised our
spirits, which, I am not ashamed to say, had all the
morning been depressed. It was not that we were not
eager to close with the enemy, but that the counter-
marching and halting ominously betokened a vacillation
of purpose in those who had the guidance of affairs.
Here in two days the invaders had got more than twenty
miles inland, and nothing effectual had been done to stop
them. And the ignorance in which we volunteers, from
the colonel downwards, were kept of their movements,
filled us with uneasiness. We could not but depict to
ourselves the enemy as carrying out all the while firmly
his well-considered scheme of attack, and contrasting it
with our own uncertainty of purpose. The very silence
with which his advance appeared to be conducted filled
us with mysterious awe. Meanwhile the day wore on,
and we became faint with hunger, for we had eaten
nothing since daybreak. No provisions came up, and
there were no signs of any commissariat officers. It
seems that when we were at the Waterloo station a whole
trainful of provisions was drawn up there, and our colonel

proposed that one of the trucks should be taken off and attached to our train, so that we might have some food at hand; but the officer in charge, an assistant-controller I think they called him—this control department was a newfangled affair which did us almost as much harm as the enemy in the long-run—said his orders were to keep all the stores together, and that he couldn't issue any without authority from the head of his department. So we had to go without. Those who had tobacco smoked—indeed there is no solace like a pipe under such circumstances. The militia regiment, I heard afterwards, had two days' provisions in their haversacks; it was we volunteers who had no haversacks, and nothing to put in them. All this time, I should tell you, while we were lying on the grass with our arms piled, the General, with the brigadiers and staff, was riding about slowly from point to point of the edge of the common, looking out with his glass towards the south valley. Orderlies and staff-officers were constantly coming, and about three o'clock there arrived up a road that led towards Horsham a small body of lancers and a regiment of yeomanry, who had, it appears, been out in advance, and now drew up a short way in front of us in column facing to the south. Whether they could see anything in their front I could not tell, for we were behind the crest of the hill ourselves, and so could not look into the valley below; but shortly afterwards the assembly sounded. Commanding officers were called out by the General, and received some brief instructions; and the column began to march again towards London, the militia this time coming last in our brigade. A rumour regarding the object of this counter-march soon spread through the ranks. The enemy was not going to attack us here, but was trying to turn the position on both sides, one column pointing to Reigate, the other to Aldershot; and so we must fall back and take up a position at Dorking. The line of the great chalk-range was to be defended. A large force was concentrating at Guildford, another at Reigate, and we should find supports at Dorking. The enemy would be awaited in these positions. Such, so far as we privates could get at the facts, was to be the plan of operations. Down the hill, therefore, we marched. From one or two points we could catch a brief sight of the railway in the valley below running from Dorking to Horsham. Men in red were working upon it here and there. They were the Royal Engineers, some one said, breaking up the line. On we marched. The dust seemed worse than ever. In one village through which we passed—I forget the name now—there was a pump on the green. Here we stopped and had a good drink; and passing by a large farm, the farmer's wife and two or three of her maids stood at the gate and handed us hunches of bread and cheese out of some baskets. I got the share of a bit, but the bottom of the good woman's baskets must soon have been reached. Not a thing else was to be had till we got to Dorking about six o'clock; indeed most of the farm-houses appeared deserted already. On arriving there we were drawn up in the street, and just opposite was a baker's shop. Our fellows asked leave at first by twos and threes to go in and buy some loaves, but soon others began to break off and crowd into the shop, and at last a regular scramble took place. If there had been any order preserved, and a regular distribution arranged, they would no doubt have been steady enough, but hunger makes men selfish; each man felt that his stopping behind would do no good—he would simply lose his share; so it ended by almost the whole regiment joining in the scrimmage, and the shop was cleared out in a couple of minutes; while as for paying, you could not get your hand into your pocket for the crush. The colonel tried in vain to stop the row; some of the officers were as bad as the men. Just then a staff-officer rode by; he could scarcely make way for the crowd, and was pushed against rather rudely, and in a passion he called out to us to behave properly, like soldiers, and not like a parcel of roughs. "Oh, blow it, governor," said Dick Wake, "you aren't agoing to come between a poor cove and his grub." Wake was an articled attorney, and, as we used to say in those days, a cheeky young chap, although a good-natured fellow enough. At this speech, which was followed by some more remarks of the sort from those about him, the staff-officer became angrier still. "Orderly," cried he to the lancer riding behind him, "take that man to the provost-marshal. As for you, sir," he said, turning to our colonel, who sat on his horse silent with astonishment, "if you don't want some of your men shot before their time, you and your precious officers had better keep this rabble in a little better order;" and poor Dick, who looked crest-fallen enough, would certainly have been led off at the tail of the sergeant's horse, if the brigadier had not come up and arranged matters, and marched us off to the hill beyond the town. This incident made us both angry and crestfallen. We were annoyed at being so roughly spoken to : at the same time we felt we had deserved it, and were ashamed of the misconduct. Then, too, we had lost confidence in our colonel, after the poor figure he cut in the affair. He was a good fellow, the colonel, and showed himself a brave one next day; but he aimed too much at being popular, and didn't understand a bit how to command.

To resume :—We had scarcely reached the hill above the town, which we were told was to be our bivouac for the night, when the welcome news came that a food-train had arrived at the station; but there were no carts to bring the things up, so a fatigue-party went down and carried back a supply to us in their arms,—loaves, a barrel of rum, packets of tea, and joints of meat—abundance for all; but there was not a kettle or a cooking-pot in the regiment, and we could not eat the meat raw. The colonel and officers were no better off. They had arranged to have a regular mess, with crockery, steward, and all complete, but the establishment never turned up, and what had become of it no one knew. Some of us were sent back into the town to see what we could procure in the way of cooking utensils. We found the street full of artillery, baggage-waggons, and mounted officers, and volunteers shopping like ourselves; and all the houses appeared to be occupied by troops. We succeeded in getting a few kettles and saucepans, and I obtained for myself a leather bag, with a strap to go over the shoulder, which proved very handy afterwards; and thus laden, we trudged back to our camp on the hill, filling the kettles with dirty water from a little stream which runs between the hill and the town, for there was none to be had above. It was nearly a couple of miles each way; and, exhausted as we were with marching and want of rest, we were almost too tired to eat. The cooking was of the roughest, as you may suppose; all we could do was to cut off slices of the meat and boil them in the saucepans, using our fingers for forks. The tea, however, was very refreshing; and, thirsty as we were, we drank it by the gallon. Just before it grew dark, the brigade-major came round, and, with the adjutant, showed our colonel how to set a picket in advance of our line a little way down the face of the hill. It was not necessary to place one, I suppose, because the town in our front was still occupied with troops; but no doubt the practice would be useful. We had also a quarter-guard, and a line of sentries in front and rear of our line, communicat-

ing with those of the regiments on our flanks. Firewood
was plentiful, for the hill was covered with beautiful
wood; but it took some time to collect it, for we had
nothing but our pocket-knives to cut down the branches
with.

So we lay down to sleep. My company had no duty,
and we had the night undisturbed to ourselves; but, tired
though I was, the excitement and the novelty of the situ-
ation made sleep difficult. And although the night was
still and warm, and we were sheltered by the woods, I
soon found it chilly with no better covering than my thin
dust-coat, the more so as my clothes, saturated with per-
spiration during the day, had never dried; and before
daylight I woke from a short nap, shivering with cold,
and was glad to get warm with others by a fire. I then
noticed that the opposite hills on the south were dotted
with fires; and we thought at first they must belong to
the enemy, but we were told that the ground up there
was still held by a strong rear-guard of regulars, and that
there need be no fear of a surprise.

At the first sign of dawn the bugles of the regiments
sounded the *reveillé*, and we were ordered to fall in, and
the roll was called. About twenty men were absent, who
had fallen out sick the day before; they had been sent
up to London by train during the night, I believe. After
standing in column for about half an hour, the brigade-
major came down with orders to pile arms and stand
easy; and perhaps half an hour afterwards we were told
to get breakfast as quickly as possible, and to cook a
day's food at the same time. This operation was managed
pretty much in the same way as the evening before, except that we had our cooking pots and kettles ready.
Meantime there was leisure to look around, and from
where we stood there was a commanding view of one of
the most beautiful scenes in England. Our regiment

was drawn up on the extremity of the ridge which runs
from Guildford to Dorking. This is indeed merely a
part of the great chalk-range which extends from beyond
Aldershot east to the Medway; but there is a gap in the
ridge just here where the little stream that runs past
Dorking turns suddenly to the north, to find its way to
the Thames. We stood on the slope of the hill, as it
trends down eastward towards this gap, and had passed
our bivouac in what appeared to be a gentleman's park.
A little way above us, and to our right, was a very fine
country-seat to which the park was attached, now occupied by the headquarters of our division. From this
house the hill sloped steeply down southward to the valley below, which runs nearly east and west parallel to
the ridge, and carries the railway and the road from
Guildford to Reigate; and in which valley, immediately
in front of the chateau, and perhaps a mile and a half
distant from it, was the little town of Dorking, nestled
in the trees, and rising up the foot of the slopes on the
other side of the valley which stretched away to Leith
Common, the scene of yesterday's march. Thus the
main part of the town of Dorking was on our right front,
but the suburbs stretched away eastward nearly to our
proper front, culminating in a small railway station, from
which the grassy slopes of the park rose up dotted with
shrubs and trees to where we were standing. Round
this railway station was a cluster of villas and one or two
mills, of whose gardens we thus had a bird's-eye view,
their little ornamental ponds glistening like looking-glasses
in the morning sun. Immediately on our left the park
sloped steeply down to the gap before mentioned, through
which ran the little stream, as well as the railway from
Epsom to Brighton, nearly due north and south, meeting
the Guildford and Reigate line at right angles. Close to
the point of intersection and the little station already

mentioned, was the station of the former line where we
had stopped the day before. Beyond the gap on the
east (our left), and in continuation of our ridge, rose the
chalk-hill again. The shoulder of this ridge overlooking
the gap is called Box Hill, from the shrubbery of box-
wood with which it was covered. Its sides were very
steep, and the top of the ridge was covered with troops.
The natural strength of our position was manifested at a
glance; a high grassy ridge steep to the south, with a
stream in front, and but little cover up the sides. It seemed
made for a battle-field. The weak point was the gap;
the ground at the junction of the railways and the roads
immediately at the entrance of the gap formed a little
valley, dotted, as I have said, with buildings and gardens.
This, in one sense, was the key of the position; for although it would not be tenable while we held the ridge
commanding it, the enemy by carrying this point and advancing through the gap would cut our line in two. But
you must not suppose I scanned the ground thus criti-
cally at the time. Anybody, indeed, might have been
struck with the natural advantages of our position; but
what, as I remember, most impressed me, was the peace-
ful beauty of the scene—the little town with the outline
of the houses obscured by a blue mist, the massive crisp-
ness of the foliage, the outlines of the great trees, lighted
up by the sun, and relieved by deep-blue shade. So
thick was the timber here, rising up the southern slopes
of the valley, that it looked almost as if it might have
been a primeval forest. The quiet of the scene was the
more impressive because contrasted in the mind with the
scenes we expected to follow; and I can remember, as
if it were yesterday, the sensation of bitter regret that it
should now be too late to avert this coming desecration
of our country, which might so easily have been prevented.
A little firmness, a little prevision on the part of our rulers,

even a little common-sense, and this great calamity would
have been rendered utterly impossible. Too late, alas!
We were like the foolish virgins in the parable.

But you must not suppose the scene immediately
around was gloomy: the camp was brisk and bustling
enough. We had got over the stress of weariness; our
stomachs were full; we felt a natural enthusiasm at the
prospect of having so soon to take a part as the real
defenders of the country, and we were inspirited at the
sight of the large force that was now assembled. Along
the slopes which trended off to the rear of our ridge,
troops came marching up—volunteers, militia, cavalry,
and guns; these, I heard, had come down from the north
as far as Leatherhead the night before, and had marched
over at daybreak. Long trains, too, began to arrive by
the rail through the gap, one after the other, containing
militia and volunteers, who moved up to the ridge to the
right and left, and took up their position, massed for the
most part on the slopes which ran up from, and in rear
of, where we stood. We now formed part of an army
corps, we were told, consisting of three divisions, but
what regiments composed the other two divisions I never
heard. All this movement we could distinctly see from
our position, for we had hurried over our breakfast,
expecting every minute that the battle would begin, and
now stood or sat about on the ground near our piled
arms. Early in the morning, too, we saw a very long
train come along the valley from the direction of Guildford, full of redcoats. It halted at the little station at
our feet, and the troops alighted. We could soon make
out their bear-skins. They were the Guards, coming to
reinforce this part of the line. Leaving a detachment of
skirmishers to hold the line of the railway embankment,
the main body marched up with a springy step and with
the band playing, and drew up across the gap on our

left, in prolongation of our line. There appeared to be three battalions of them, for they formed up in that number of columns at short intervals.

Shortly after this I was sent over to Box Hill with a message from our colonel to the colonel of a volunteer regiment stationed there, to know whether an ambulance-cart was obtainable, as it was reported this regiment was well supplied with carriage, whereas we were without any: my mission, however, was futile. Crossing the valley, I found a scene of great confusion at the railway station. Trains were still coming in with stores, ammunition, guns, and appliances of all sorts, which were being unloaded as fast as possible; but there were scarcely any means of getting the things off. There were plenty of waggons of all sorts, but hardly any horses to draw them, and the whole place was blocked up; while, to add to the confusion, a regular exodus had taken place of the people from the town, who had been warned that it was likely to be the scene of fighting. Ladies and women of all sorts and ages, and children, some with bundles, some empty-handed, were seeking places in the train, but there appeared no one on the spot authorised to grant them, and these poor creatures were pushing their way up and down, vainly asking for information and permission to get away. In the crowd I observed our surgeon, who likewise was in search of an ambulance of some sort: his whole professional apparatus, he said, consisted of a case of instruments. Also in the crowd I stumbled upon Wood, Travers's old coachman. He had been sent down by his mistress to Guildford, because it was supposed our regiment had gone there, riding the horse, and laden with a supply of things—food, blankets, and, of course, a letter. He had also brought my knapsack; but at Guildford the horse was pressed for artillery work, and a receipt for it given him in exchange, so he had been

obliged to leave all the heavy packages there, including
my knapsack; but the faithful old man had brought on
as many things as he could carry, and hearing that we
should be found in this part, had walked over thus laden
from Guildford. He said that place was crowded with
troops, and that the heights were lined with them the
whole way between the two towns; also, that some trains
with wounded had passed up from the coast in the night,
through Guildford. I led him off to where our regiment
was, relieving the old man from part of the load he was
staggering under. The food sent was not now so much
needed, but the plates, knives, &c., and drinking-vessels,
promised to be handy—and Travers, you may be sure,
was delighted to get his letter; while a couple of news-
papers the old man had brought were eagerly competed
for by all, even at this critical moment, for we had heard
no authentic news since we left London on Sunday.
And even at this distance of time, although I only
glanced down the paper, I can remember almost the
very words I read there. They were both copies of the
same paper: the first, published on Sunday evening,
when the news had arrived of the successful landing at
three points, was written in a tone of despair. The
country must confess that it had been taken by surprise.
The conqueror would be satisfied with the humiliation
inflicted by a peace dictated on our own shores; it was
the clear duty of the Government to accept the best terms
obtainable, and to avoid further bloodshed and disaster,
and avert the fall of our tottering mercantile credit. The
next morning's issue was in quite a different tone. Apparently the enemy had received a check, for we were
here exhorted to resistance. An impregnable position
was to be taken up along the Downs, a force was concentrating there far outnumbering the rash invaders,
who, with an invincible line before them, and the sea

behind, had no choice between destruction or surrender. Let there be no pusillanimous talk of negotiation, the fight must be fought out; and there could be but one issue. England, expectant but calm, awaited with confidence the result of the attack on its unconquerable volunteers. The writing appeared to me eloquent, but rather inconsistent. The same paper said the Government had sent off 500 workmen from Woolwich, to open a branch arsenal at Birmingham.

All this time we had nothing to do, except to change our position, which we did every few minutes, now moving up the hill farther to our right, now taking ground lower down to our left, as one order after another was brought down the line ; but the staff-officers were galloping about perpetually with orders, while the rumble of the artillery as they moved about from one part of the field to another went on almost incessantly. At last the whole line stood to arms, the bands struck up, and the general commanding our army corps came riding down with his staff. We had seen him several times before, as we had been moving frequently about the position during the morning ; but he now made a sort of formal inspection. He was a tall thin man, with long light hair, very well mounted, and as he sat his horse with an erect seat, and came prancing down the line, at a little distance he looked as if he might be five-and-twenty ; but I believe he had served more than fifty years, and had been made a peer for services performed when quite an old man. I remember that he had more decorations than there was room for on the breast of his coat, and wore them suspended like a necklace round his neck. Like all the other generals, he was dressed in blue, with a cocked-hat and feathers—a bad plan, I thought, for it made them very conspicuous. The general halted before·our battalion, and after looking at us a while, made a short address : We had a post of honour next her Majesty's Guards, and would show ourselves worthy of it, and of the name of Englishmen. It did not need, he said, to be a general to see the strength of our position; it was impregnable, if properly held. Let us wait till the enemy was well pounded, and then the word would be given to go at him. Above everything, we must be steady. He then shook hands with our colonel, we gave him a cheer, and he rode on to where the Guards were drawn up.

Now then, we thought, the battle will begin. But still there were no signs of the enemy ; and the air, though hot and sultry, began to be very hazy, so that you could scarcely see the town below, and the hills opposite were merely a confused blur, in which no features could be distinctly made out. After a while, the tension of feeling which followed the general's address relaxed, and we began to feel less as if everything depended on keeping our rifles firmly grasped: we were told to pile arms again, and got leave to go down by tens and twenties to the stream below to drink. This stream, and all the hedges and banks on our side of it, were held by our skirmishers, but the town had been abandoned. The position appeared an excellent one, except that the enemy, when they came, would have almost better cover than our men. While I was down at the brook, a column emerged from the town, making for our position. We thought for a moment it was the enemy, and you could not make out the colour of the uniforms for the dust; but it turned out to be our rearguard, falling back from the opposite hills which they had occupied the previous night. One battalion, of rifles, halted for a few minutes at the stream to let the men drink, and I had a minute's talk with a couple of the officers. They had formed part of the force which had attacked the enemy on their first landing. They had it all their own way, they said, at first, and could have beaten the enemy back easily if they had been properly supported; but the whole thing was mismanaged. The volunteers came on very pluckily, they said, but they got into confusion, and so did the militia, and the attack failed with serious loss. It was the wounded of this force which had passed through Guildford in the night. The officers asked us eagerly about the arrangements for the battle, and when we said that the Guards were the only regular troops in this part of the field, shook their heads ominously.

While we were talking, a third officer came up; he was a dark man with a smooth face and a curious excited manner. "You are volunteers, I suppose," he said, quickly, his eye flashing the while. "Well, now, look here; mind I don't want to hurt your feelings, or to say anything unpleasant, but I'll tell you what; if all you gentlemen were just to go back, and leave us to fight it out alone, it would be a devilish good thing. We could do it a precious deal better without you, I assure you. We don't want your help, I can tell you. We would much rather be left alone, I assure you. Mind I don't want to say anything rude, but that's a fact." Having blurted out this passionately, he strode away before any one could reply, or the other officers could stop him. They apologised for his rudeness, saying that his brother, also in the regiment, had been killed on Sunday, and that this, and the sun, and marching, had affected his head. The officers told us that the enemy's advanced-guard was close behind, but that he had apparently been waiting for reinforcements, and would probably not attack in force until noon. It was, however, nearly three o'clock before the battle began. We had almost worn out the feeling of expectancy. For

twelve hours had we been waiting for the coming struggle, till at last it seemed almost as if the invasion were
but a bad dream, and the enemy, as yet unseen by us,
had no real existence. So far things had not been very
different, but for the numbers and for what we had been
told, from a Volunteer review on Brighton Downs. I
remember that these thoughts were passing through my
mind as we lay down in groups on the grass, some smoking, some nibbling at their bread, some even asleep,
when the listless state we had fallen into was suddenly
disturbed by a gunshot fired from the top of the hill on
our right, close by the big house. It was the first time
I had ever heard a shotted gun fired, and although it is
fifty years ago, the angry whistle of the shot as it left the
gun is in my ears now. The sound was soon to become
common enough. We all jumped up at the report, and
fell in almost without the word being given, grasping
our rifles tightly, and the leading files peering forward to
look for the approaching enemy. This gun was apparently the signal to begin, for now our batteries opened
fire all along the line. What they were firing at I could
not see, and I am sure the gunners could not see much
themselves. I have told you what a haze had come
over the air since the morning, and now the smoke from
the guns settled like a pall over the hill, and soon we
could see little but the men in our ranks, and the outline of some gunners in the battery drawn up next us on
the slope on our right. This firing went on, I should
think, for nearly a couple of hours, and still there was no
reply. We could see the gunners—it was a troop of
horse-artillery—working away like fury, ramming, load-
ing, and running up with cartridges, the officer in command riding slowly up and down just behind his guns,
and peering out with his field-glass into the mist. Once
or twice they ceased firing to let their smoke clear away,

but this did not do much good. For nearly two hours did this go on, and not a shot came in reply. If a battle is like this, said Dick Wake, who was my next-hand file, it's mild work, to say the least. The words were hardly uttered when a rattle of musketry was heard in front; our skirmishers were at it, and very soon the bullets began to sing over our heads, and some struck the ground at our feet. Up to this time we had been in column; we were now deployed into line on the ground assigned to us. From the valley or gap on our left there ran a lane right up the hill almost due west, or along our front. This lane had a thick bank about four feet high, and the greater part of the regiment was drawn up behind it; but a little way up the hill the lane trended back out of the line, so the right of the regiment here left it and occupied the open grass-land of the park. The bank had been cut away at this point to admit of our going in and out. We had been told in the morning to cut down the bushes on the top of the bank, so as to make the space clear for firing over, but we had no tools to work with; however, a party of sappers had come down and finished the job. My company was on the right, and was thus beyond the shelter of the friendly bank. On our right again was the battery of artillery already mentioned; then came a battalion of the line, then more guns, then a great mass of militia and volunteers and a few line up to the big house. At least this was the order before the firing began; after that I do not know what changes took place.

And now the enemy's artillery began to open; where their guns were posted we could not see, but we began to hear the rush of the shells over our heads, and the bang as they burst just beyond. And now what took place I can really hardly tell you. Sometimes when I try and recall the scene, it seems as if it lasted for only a few minutes; yet I know, as we lay on the ground, I thought the hours would never pass away, as we watched the gunners still plying their task, firing at the invisible enemy, never stopping for a moment except when now and again a dull blow would be heard and a man fall down, then three or four of his comrades would carry him to the rear. The captain no longer rode up and down; what had become of him I do not know. Two of the guns ceased firing for a time; they had got injured in some way, and up rode an artillery general. I think I see him now, a very handsome man, with straight features and a dark mustache, his breast covered with medals. He appeared in a great rage at the guns stopping fire.

" Who commands this battery ? " he cried.

" I do, Sir Henry," said an officer, riding forward, whom I had not noticed before.

The group is before me at this moment, standing out clear against the background of smoke, Sir Henry erect on his splendid charger, his flashing eye, his left arm pointing towards the enemy to enforce something he was going to say, the young officer reining in his horse just beside him, and saluting with his right hand raised to his busby. This for a moment, then a dull thud, and both horses and riders are prostrate on the ground. A round-shot had struck all four at the saddle-line. Some of the gunners ran up to help, but neither officer could have lived many minutes. This was not the first I saw killed. Some time before this, almost immediately on the enemy's artillery opening, as we were lying, I heard something like the sound of metal striking metal, and at the same moment Dick Wake, who was next me in the ranks, leaning on his elbows, sank forward on his face. I looked round and saw what had happened ; a shot fired at a high elevation, passing over his head, had

struck the ground behind, nearly cutting his thigh off.
It must have been the ball striking his sheathed bayonet
which made the noise. Three of us carried the poor
fellow to the rear, with difficulty for the shattered limb;
but he was nearly dead from loss of blood when we got
to the doctor, who was waiting in a sheltered hollow
about two hundred yards in rear, with two other doctors in
plain clothes, who had come up to help., We deposited
our burden and returned to the front. Poor Wake was
sensible when we left him, but apparently too shaken by
the shock to be able to speak. Wood was there helping
the doctors. I paid more visits to the rear of the same
sort before the evening was over.

All this time we were lying there to be fired at without
returning a shot, for our skirmishers were holding the line
of walls and enclosures below. However, the bank protected most of us, and the brigadier now ordered our
right company, which was in the open, to get behind it
also; and there we lay about four deep, the shells crashing and bullets whistling over our heads, but hardly
a man being touched. Our colonel was, indeed, the only
one exposed, for he rode up and down the lane at a foot-
pace as steady as a rock; but he made the major and
adjutant dismount, and take shelter behind the hedge,
holding their horses. We were all pleased to see him so
cool, and it restored our confidence in him, which had
been shaken yesterday.

The time seemed interminable while we lay thus in-
active. We could not, of course, help peering over the
bank to try and see what was going on; but there was
nothing to be made out, for now a tremendous thunder-
storm, which had been gathering all day, burst on us,
and a torrent of almost blinding rain came down, which
obscured the view even more than the smoke, while the
crashing of the thunder and the glare of the lightning

could be heard and seen even above the roar and flashing of the artillery. Once the mist lifted, and I saw for
a minute an attack on Box Hill, on the other side of the
gap on our left. It was like the scene at a theatre—a
curtain of smoke all round and a clear gap in the centre,
with a sudden gleam of evening sunshine lighting it up.
The steep smooth slope of the hill was crowded with the
dark-blue figures of the enemy, whom I now saw for the
first time—an irregular outline in front, but very solid in
rear: the whole body was moving forward by fits and
starts, the men firing and advancing, the officers waving
their swords, the columns closing up and gradually making
way. Our people were almost concealed by the bushes
at the top, whence the smoke and their fire could be seen
proceeding: presently from these bushes on the crest
came out a red line, and dashed down the brow of the
hill, a flame of fire belching out from the front as it advanced. The enemy hesitated, gave way, and finally ran
back in a confused crowd down the hill. Then the mist
covered the scene, but the glimpse of this splendid
charge was inspiriting, and I hoped we should show the
same coolness when it came to our turn. It was about
this time that our skirmishers fell back, a good many
wounded, some limping along by themselves, others
helped. The main body retired in very fair order, halting to turn round and fire; we could see a mounted
officer of the Guards riding up and down encouraging
them to be steady. Now came our turn. For a few
minutes we saw nothing, but a rattle of bullets came
through the rain and mist, mostly, however, passing
over the bank. We began to fire in reply, stepping up
against the bank to fire, and stooping down to load; but
our brigade-major rode up with an order, and the word
was passed through the men to reserve our fire. In a
very few moments it must have been that, when ordered

to stand up, we could see the helmet-spikes and then the figures of the skirmishers as they came on : a lot of them there appeared to be, five or six deep I should say, but in loose order, each man stopping to aim and fire, and then coming forward a little. Just then the brigadier clattered on horseback up the lane. " Now, then, gentlemen, give it them hot!" he cried ; and fire away we did, as fast as ever we were able. A perfect storm of bullets seemed to be flying about us too, and I thought each moment must be the last ; escape seemed impossible, but I saw no one fall, for I was too busy, and so were we all, to look to the right or left, but loaded and fired as fast as we could. How long this went on I know not—it could not have been long ; neither side could have lasted many minutes under such a fire, but it ended by the enemy gradually falling back, and as soon as we saw this we raised a tremendous shout, and some of us jumped up on the bank to give them our parting shots. Suddenly the order was passed down the line to cease firing, and we soon discovered the cause; a battalion of the Guards was charging obliquely across from our left across our front. It was, I expect, their flank attack as much as our fire which had turned back the enemy ; and it was a splendid sight to see their steady line as they advanced slowly across the smooth lawn below us, firing as they went, but as steady as if on parade. We felt a great elation at this moment ; it seemed as if the battle was won. Just then somebody called out to look to the wounded, and for the first time I turned to glance down the rank along the lane. Then I saw that we had not beaten back the attack without loss. Immediately before me lay Bob Lawford of my office, dead on his back from a bullet through his forehead, his hand still grasping his rifle. At every step was some friend or acquaintance killed or wounded, and a few paces down the lane I found Travers, sitting with his back against the bank. A ball had gone through his lungs, and blood was coming from his mouth. I was lifting him up, but the cry of agony he gave stopped me. I then saw that this was not his only wound; his thigh was smashed by a bullet (which must have hit him when standing on the bank), and the blood streaming down mixed in a muddy puddle with the rain-water under him. Still he could not be left here, so, lifting him up as well as I could, I carried him through the gate which led out of the lane at the back to where our camp hospital was in the rear. The movement must have caused him awful agony, for I could not support the broken thigh, and he could not restrain his groans, brave fellow though he was; but how I carried him at all I cannot make out, for he was a much bigger man than myself; but I had not gone far, one of a stream of our fellows, all on the same errand, when a bandsman and Wood met me, bringing a hurdle as a stretcher, and on this we placed him. Wood had just time to tell me that he had got a cart down in the hollow, and would endeavour to take off his master at once to Kingston, when a staff-officer rode up to call us to the ranks. "You really must not straggle in this way, gentlemen," he said; "pray keep your ranks." "But we can't leave our wounded to be trodden down and die," cried one of our fellows. "Beat off the enemy first, sir," he replied. "Gentlemen, do, pray, join your regiments, or we shall be a regular mob." And no doubt he did not speak too soon; for besides our fellows straggling to the rear, lots of volunteers from the regiments in reserve were running forward to help, till the whole ground was dotted with groups of men. I hastened back to my post, but I had just time to notice that all the ground in our rear was occupied by a thick mass of troops, much more numerous than in the morning, and a column was moving down to the left of our line, to the ground before held by the Guards. All this time, although the musketry had slackened, the artillery-fire seemed heavier than ever; the shells screamed overhead or burst around; and I confess to feeling quite a relief at getting back to the friendly shelter of the lane. Looking over the bank, I noticed for the first time the frightful execution our fire had created. The space in front was thickly strewed with dead and badly wounded, and beyond the bodies of the fallen enemy could just be seen—for it was now getting dusk—the bear-skins and red coats of our own gallant Guards scattered over the slope, and marking the line of their victorious advance. But hardly a minute could have passed in thus looking over the field, when our brigade-major came moving up the lane on foot (I suppose his horse had been shot), crying, "Stand to your arms, volunteers! they're coming on again;" and we found ourselves a second time engaged in a hot musketry-fire. How long it went on I cannot now remember, but we could distinguish clearly the thick line of skirmishers, about sixty paces off, and mounted officers among them; and we seemed to be keeping them well in check, for they were quite exposed to our fire, while we were protected nearly up to our shoulders, when—I know not how—I became sensible that something had gone wrong. "We are taken in flank!" called out some one; and looking along the left, sure enough there were dark figures jumping over the bank into the lane and firing up along our line. The volunteers in reserve, who had come down to take the place of the Guards, must have given way at this point; the enemy's skirmishers had got through our line, and turned our left flank. How the next move came about I cannot recollect, or whether it was without orders, but in a short time we found ourselves out of the lane, and drawn up in a strag-

gling line about thirty yards in rear of it—at our end,
that is, the other flank had fallen back a good deal more
—and the enemy were lining the hedge, and numbers of
them passing over and forming up on our side. Beyond
our left a confused mass were retreating, firing as they
went, followed by the advancing line of the enemy. We
stood in this way for a short space, firing at random as
fast as we could. Our colonel and major must have
been shot, for there was no one to give an order, when
somebody on horseback called out from behind—I think
it must have been the brigadier—" Now, then, volunteers! give a British cheer, and go at them—charge!"
and, with a shout, we rushed at the enemy. Some of
them ran, some stopped to meet us, and for a moment
it was a real hand-to-hand fight. I felt a sharp sting in
my leg, as I drove my bayonet right through the man in
front of me. I confess I shut my eyes, for I just got a
glimpse of the poor wretch as he fell back, his eyes
starting out of his head, and, savage though we were,
the sight was almost too horrible to look at. But the
struggle was over in a second, and we had cleared the
ground again right up to the rear hedge of the lane. Had
we gone on, I believe we might have recovered the lane
too, but we were now all out of order; there was no one to
say what to do; the enemy began to line the hedge and
open fire, and they were streaming past our left; and how
it came about I know not, but we found ourselves falling
back towards our right rear, scarce any semblance of a
line remaining, and the volunteers who had given way
on our left mixed up with us, and adding to the confusion. It was now nearly dark. On the slopes which we
were retreating to was a large mass of reserves drawn up
in columns. Some of the leading files of these, mistak-
ing us for the enemy, began firing at us; our fellows,
crying out to them to stop, ran towards their ranks, and

in a few moments the whole slope of the hill became a
scene of confusion that I cannot attempt to describe,
regiments and detachments mixed up in hopeless dis-
order. Most of us, I believe, turned towards the enemy
and fired away our few remaining cartridges; but it was
too late to take aim, fortunately for us, or the guns which
the enemy had brought up through the gap, and were
firing point-blank, would have done more damage. As
it was, we could see little more than the bright flashes of
their fire. In our confusion we had jammed up a line
regiment immediately behind us, which I suppose had
just arrived on the field, and its colonel and some
staff-officers were in vain trying to make a passage for
it, and their shouts to us to march to the rear and
clear a road could be heard above the roar of the guns
and the confused babel of sound. At last a mounted
officer pushed his way through, followed by a company
in sections, the men brushing past with firm-set faces, as
if on a desperate task; and the battalion, when it got
clear, appeared to deploy and advance down the slope.
I have also a dim recollection of seeing the Life Guards
trot past the front, and push on towards the town—a last
desperate attempt to save the day—before we left the
field. Our adjutant, who had got separated from our
flank of the regiment in the confusion, now came up, and
managed to lead us, or at any rate some of us, up to the
crest of the hill in the rear, to re-form, as he said; but
there we met a vast crowd of volunteers, militia, and
waggons, all hurrying rearward from the direction of the
big house, and we were borne in the stream for a mile at
least before it was possible to stop. At last the adjutant
led us to an open space a little off the line of fugitives,
and there we re-formed the remains of the companies.
Telling us to halt, he rode off to try and obtain orders,
and find out where the rest of our brigade was. From

this point, a spur of high ground running off from the main plateau, we looked down through the dim twilight into the battle-field below. Artillery-fire was still going on. We could see the flashes from the guns on both sides, and now and then a stray shell came screaming up and burst near us, but we were beyond the sound of musketry. This halt first gave us time to think about what had happened. The long day of expectancy had been succeeded by the excitement of battle; and when each minute may be your last, you do not think much about other people, nor when you are facing another man with a rifle have you time to consider whether he or you are the invader, or that you are fighting for your home and hearths. All fighting is pretty much alike, I suspect, as to sentiment, when once it begins. But now we had time for reflection; and although we did not yet quite understand how far the day had gone against us, an uneasy feeling of self-condemnation must have come up in the minds of most of us; while, above all, we now began to realise what the loss of this battle meant to the country. Then, too, we knew not what had become of all our wounded comrades. Reaction, too, set in after the fatigue and excitement. For myself, I had found out for the first time that besides the bayonet-wound in my leg, a bullet had gone through my left arm, just below the shoulder, and outside the bone. I remember feeling something like a blow just when we lost the lane, but the wound passed unnoticed till now, when the bleeding had stopped and the shirt was sticking to the wound.

This half-hour seemed an age, and while we stood on this knoll the endless tramp of men and rumbling of carts along the downs beside us told their own tale. The whole army was falling back. At last we could discern the adjutant riding up to us out of the dark. The army was to retreat and take up a position on Epsom Downs,

he said; we should join in the march, and try and find
our brigade in the morning; and so we turned into the
throng again, and made our way on as best we could.
A few scraps of news he gave us as he rode alongside of
our leading section; the army had held its position well
for a time, but the enemy had at last broken through the
line between us and Guildford, as well as in our front,
and had poured his men through the point gained, throw-
ing the line into confusion, and the first army corps near
Guildford were also falling back to avoid being out-
flanked. The regular troops were holding the rear; we
were to push on as fast as possible to get out of their
way, and allow them to make an orderly retreat in the
morning. The gallant old lord commanding our corps
had been badly wounded early in the day, he heard, and
carried off the field. The Guards had suffered dreadfully; the household cavalry had ridden down the cuiras-
siers, but had got into broken ground and been awfully
cut up. Such were the scraps of news passed down our
weary column. What had become of our wounded no
one knew, and no one liked to ask. So we trudged on.
It must have been midnight when we reached Leatherhead. Here we left the open ground and took to the
road, and the block became greater. We pushed our way
painfully along; several trains passed slowly ahead along
the railway by the roadside, containing the wounded, we
supposed—such of them, at least, as were lucky enough
to be picked up. It was daylight when we got to Epsom.
The night had been bright and clear after the storm, with
a cool air, which, blowing through my soaking clothes,
chilled me to the bone. My wounded leg was stiff and
sore, and I was ready to drop with exhaustion and hunger.
Nor were my comrades in much better case; we had
eaten nothing since breakfast the day before, and the
bread we had put by had been washed away by the

storm: only a little pulp remained at the bottom of my bag. The tobacco was all too wet to smoke. In this plight we were creeping along, when the adjutant guided us into a field by the roadside to rest awhile, and we lay down exhausted on the sloppy grass. The roll was here taken, and only 180 answered out of nearly 500 present on the morning of the battle. How many of these were killed and wounded no one could tell; but it was certain many must have got separated in the confusion of the evening. While resting here, we saw pass by, in the crowd of vehicles and men, a cart laden with commissariat stores, driven by a man in uniform. " Food !" cried some one, and a dozen volunteers jumped up and surrounded the cart. The driver tried to whip them off; but he was pulled off his seat, and the contents of the cart thrown out in an instant. They were preserved meats in tins, which we tore open with our bayonets. The meat had been cooked before, I think; at any rate we devoured it. Shortly after this a general came by with three or four staff-officers. He stopped and spoke to our adjutant, and then rode into the field. " My lads," said he, " you shall join my division for the present : fall in, and follow the regiment that is now passing." We rose up, fell in by companies, each about twenty strong, and turned once more into the stream moving along the road ;—regiments, detachments, single volunteers or militiamen, country people making off, some with bundles, some without, a few in carts, but most on foot; here and there waggons of stores, with men sitting wherever there was room, others crammed with wounded soldiers. Many blocks occurred from horses falling, or carts breaking down and filling up the road. In the town the confusion was even worse, for all the houses seemed full of volunteers and militiamen, wounded or resting, or trying to find food, and the streets were almost choked up. Some officers were in vain trying to restore order, but the task seemed a hopeless one. One or two volunteer regiments which had arrived from the north the previous night, and had been halted here for orders, were drawn up along the roadside steadily enough, and some of the retreating regiments, including ours, may have preserved the semblance of discipline, but for the most part the mass pushing to the rear was a mere mob. The regulars, or what remained of them, were now, I believe, all in the rear, to hold the advancing enemy in check. A few officers among such a crowd could do nothing. To add to the confusion, several houses were being emptied of the wounded brought here the night before, to prevent their falling into the hands of the enemy, some in carts, some being carried to the railway by men. The groans of these poor fellows as they were jostled through the street went to our hearts, selfish though fatigue and suffering had made us. At last, following the guidance of a staff-officer who was standing to show the way, we turned off from the main London road and took that towards Kingston. Here the crush was less, and we managed to move along pretty steadily. The air had been cooled by the storm, and there was no dust. We passed through a village where our new general had seized all the public-houses, and taken possession of the liquor; and each regiment as it came up was halted, and each man got a drink of beer, served out by companies. Whether the owner got paid, I know not, but it was like nectar. It must have been about one o'clock in the afternoon that we came in sight of Kingston. We had been on our legs sixteen hours, and had got over about twelve miles of ground. There is a hill a little south of the Surbiton station, covered then mostly with villas, but open at the western extremity, where there was a clump of trees on the summit. We had diverged from the road towards this,

and here the general halted us and disposed the line
of the division along his front, facing to the south-west,
the right of the line reaching down to the water-works
on the Thames, the left extending along the southern
slope of the hill, in the direction of the Epsom road
by which we had come. We were nearly in the centre,
occupying the knoll just in front of the general, who
dismounted on the top and tied his horse to a tree. It
is not much of a hill, but commands an extensive view
over the flat country around; and as we lay wearily
on the ground we could see the Thames glistening
like a silver field in the bright sunshine, the palace at
Hampton Court, the bridge at Kingston, and the old
church tower rising above the haze of the town, with the
woods of Richmond Park behind it. To most of us the
scene could not but call up the associations of happy
days of peace—days now ended and peace destroyed
through national infatuation. We did not say this to
each other, but a deep depression had come upon us,
partly due to weakness and fatigue, no doubt, but we
saw that another stand was going to be made, and we had
no longer any confidence in ourselves. If we could not
hold our own when stationary in line, on a good position,
but had been broken up into a rabble at the first shock,
what chance had we now of manœuvring against a victorious enemy in this open ground? A feeling of des-
peration came over us, a determination to struggle on
against hope; but anxiety for the future of the country,
and our friends, and all dear to us, filled our thoughts
now that we had time for reflection. We had had no
news of any kind since Wood joined us the day before—
we knew not what was doing in London, or what the
Government was about, or anything else; and exhausted
though we were, we felt an intense craving to know what
was happening in other parts of the country.

Our general had expected to find a supply of food and ammunition here, but nothing turned up. Most of us had hardly a cartridge left, so he ordered the regiment next to us, which came from the north and had not been engaged, to give us enough to make up twenty rounds a man, and he sent off a fatigue-party to Kingston to try and get provisions, while a detachment of our fellows was allowed to go foraging among the villas in our rear; and in about an hour they brought back some bread and meat, which gave us a slender meal all round. They said most of the houses were empty, and that many had been stripped of all eatables, and a good deal damaged already.

It must have been between three and four o'clock when the sound of cannonading began to be heard in the front, and we could see the smoke of the guns rising above the woods of Esher and Claremont, and soon afterwards some troops emerged from the fields below us. It was the rear-guard of regular troops. There were some guns also, which were driven up the slope and took up their position round the knoll. There were three batteries, but they only counted eight guns amongst them. Behind them was posted the line; it was a brigade apparently of four regiments, but the whole did not look to be more than eight or nine hundred men. Our regiment and another had been moved a little to the rear to make way for them, and presently we were ordered down to occupy the railway station on our right rear. My leg was now so stiff I could no longer march with the rest, and my left arm was very swollen and sore, and almost useless; but anything seemed better than being left behind, so I limped after the battalion as best I could down to the station. There was a goods shed a little in advance of it down the line, a strong brick building, and here my company was posted. The rest of our men lined the wall of the enclosure. A staff-officer came with us to arrange the distribution; we should be supported by line troops, he said; and in a few minutes a train full of them came slowly up from Guildford way. It was the last; the men got out, the train passed on, and a party began to tear up the rails, while the rest were distributed among the houses on each side. A sergeant's party joined us in our shed, and an engineer officer with sappers came to knock holes in the walls for us to fire from; but there were only half-a-dozen of them, so progress was not rapid, and as we had no tools we could not help.

It was while we were watching this job that the adjutant, who was as active as ever, looked in, and told us to muster in the yard. The fatigue-party had come back from Kingston, and a small baker's hand-cart of food was made over to us as our share. It contained loaves, flour, and some joints of meat. The meat and the flour we had not time or means to cook. The loaves we devoured; and there was a tap of water in the yard, so we felt refreshed by the meal. I should have liked to wash my wounds, which were becoming very offensive, but I dared not take off my coat, feeling sure I should not be able to get it on again. It was while we were eating our bread that the rumour first reached us of another disaster, even greater than that we had witnessed ourselves. Whence it came I know not; but a whisper went down the ranks that Woolwich had been captured. We all knew that it was our only arsenal, and understood the significance of the blow. No hope, if this were true, of saving the country. Thinking over this, we went back to the shed.

Although this was only our second day of war, I think we were already old soldiers so far that we had come to be careless about fire, and the shot and shell that now began to open on us made no sensation. We felt, indeed, our need of discipline, and we saw plainly enough the

slender chance of success coming out of troops so imper-
fectly trained as we were ; but I think we were all determined to fight on as long as we could. Our gallant
adjutant gave his spirit to everybody ; and the staff-
officer commanding was a very cheery fellow, and went
about as if we were certain of victory. Just as the firing
began he looked in to say that we were as safe as in a
church, that we must be sure and pepper the enemy
well, and that more cartridges would soon arrive. There
were some steps and benches in the shed, and on these
a part of our men were standing, to fire through the
upper loop-holes, while the line soldiers and others stood
on the ground, guarding the second row. I sat on the
floor, for I could not now use my rifle, and besides, there
were more men than loop-holes. The artillery fire
which had opened now on our position was from a long-
ish range ; and occupation for the riflemen had hardly
begun when there was a crash in the shed, and I was
knocked down by a blow on the head. I was almost
stunned for a time, and could not make out at first
what had happened. A shot or shell had hit the shed
without quite penetrating the wall, but the blow had
upset the steps resting against it, and the men standing
on them, bringing down a cloud of plaster and brickbats,
one of which had struck me. I felt now past being of
use. I could not use my rifle, and could barely stand ;
and after a time I thought I would make for my own
house, on the chance of finding some one still there. I
got up therefore, and staggered homewards. Musketry
fire had now commenced, and our side were blazing
away from the windows of the houses, and from behind
walls, and from the shelter of some trucks still standing in the station. A couple of field-pieces in the yard
were firing, and in the open space in rear of the station
a reserve was drawn up. There, too, was the staff-

officer on horseback, watching the fight through his
field-glass. I remember having still enough sense to
feel that the position was a hopeless one. That straggling line of houses and gardens would surely be broken
through at some point, and then the line must give way
like a rope of sand. It was about a mile to our house,
and I was thinking how I could possibly drag myself so
far when I suddenly recollected that I was passing
Travers's house,—one of the first of a row of villas then
leading from the Surbiton station to Kingston. Had
he been brought home, I wonder, as his faithful old servant promised, and was his wife still here? I remember
to this day the sensation of shame I felt, when I recollected that I had not once given him—my greatest friend
—a thought since I carried him off the field the day
before. But war and suffering make men selfish. I
would go in now at any rate and rest awhile, and see if I
could be of use. The little garden before the house was
as trim as ever—I used to pass it every day on my way
to the train, and knew every shrub in it—and ablaze with
flowers, but the hall-door stood ajar. I stepped in and
saw little Arthur standing in the hall. He had been
dressed as neatly as ever that day, and as he stood there
in his pretty blue frock and white trousers and socks
showing his chubby little legs, with his golden locks, fair
face, and large dark eyes, the picture of childish beauty,
in the quiet hall, just as it used to look—the vases of
flowers, the hat and coats hanging up, the familiar
pictures on the walls—this vision of peace in the midst
of war made me wonder for a moment, faint and giddy
as I was, if the pandemonium outside had any real
existence, and was not merely a hideous dream. But
the roar of the guns making the house shake, and the
rushing of the shot, gave a ready answer. The little
fellow appeared almost unconscious of the scene around

him, and was walking up the stairs holding by the railing, one step at a time, as I had seen him do a hundred times before, but turned round as I came in. My appearance frightened him, and staggering as I did into the hall, my face and clothes covered with blood and dirt, I must have looked an awful object to the child, for he gave a cry and turned to run toward the basement stairs. But he stopped on hearing my voice calling him back to his god-papa, and after a while came timidly up to me. Papa had been to the battle, he said, and was very ill: mamma was with papa: Wood was out: Lucy was in the cellar, and had taken him there, but he wanted to go to mamma. Telling him to stay in the hall for a minute till I called him, I climbed up-stairs and opened the bedroom-door. My poor friend lay there, his body resting on the bed, his head supported on his wife's shoulder as she sat by the bedside. He breathed heavily, but the pallor of his face, the closed eyes, the prostrate arms, the clammy foam she was wiping from his mouth, all spoke of approaching death. The good old servant had done his duty, at least, —he had brought his master home to die in his wife's arms. The poor woman was too intent on her charge to notice the opening of the door, and as the child would be better away, I closed it gently and went down to the hall to take little Arthur to the shelter below, where the maid was hiding. Too late! He lay at the foot of the stairs on his face, his little arms stretched out, his hair dabbled in blood. I had not noticed the crash among the other noises, but a splinter of a shell must have come through the open doorway; it had carried away the back of his head. The poor child's death must have been instantaneous. I tried to lift up the little corpse with my one arm, but even this load was too much for me, and while stooping down I fainted away.

When I came to my senses again it was quite dark, and for some time I could not make out where I was; I lay indeed for some time like one half asleep, feeling no inclination to move. By degrees I became aware that I was on the carpeted floor of a room. All noise of battle had ceased, but there was a sound as of many people close by. At last I sat up and gradually got to my feet. The movement gave me intense pain, for my wounds were now highly inflamed, and my clothes sticking to them made them dreadfully sore. At last I got up and groped my way to the door, and opening it at once saw where I was, for the pain had brought back my senses. I had been lying in Travers's little writing-room at the end of the passage, into which I made my way. There was no gas, and the drawing-room door was closed; but from the open dining-room the glimmer of a candle feebly lighted up the hall, in which half-a-dozen sleeping figures could be discerned, while the room itself was crowded with men. The table was covered with plates, glasses, and bottles; but most of the men were asleep in the chairs or on the floor, a few were smoking cigars, and one or two with their helmets on were still engaged at supper, occasionally grunting out an observation between the mouthfuls.

"Sind wackere Soldaten, diese Englischen Freiwilligen," said a broad-shouldered brute, stuffing a great hunch of beef into his mouth with a silver fork, an implement I should think he must have been using for the first time in his life.

"Ja, ja," replied a comrade, who was lolling back in his chair with a pair of very dirty legs on the table, and one of poor Travers's best cigars in his mouth; "Sie so gut laufen können."

"Ja wohl," responded the first speaker; "aber sind nicht eben so schnell wie die Französischen Mobloten."

"Gewiss," grunted a hulking lout from the floor, leaning on his elbow, and sending out a cloud of smoke from his ugly jaws; "und da sind hier etwa gute Schützen."

"Hast recht, lange Peter," answered number one; "wenn die Schurken so gut exerciren wie schützen könnten, so wären wir heute nicht hier!"

"Recht! recht!" said the second; "das exerciren macht den guten Soldaten."

What more criticisms on the shortcomings of our unfortunate volunteers might have passed I did not stop to hear, being interrupted by a sound on the stairs. Mrs Travers was standing on the landing-place; I limped up the stairs to meet her. Among the many pictures of those fatal days engraven on my memory, I remember none more clearly than the mournful aspect of my poor friend, widowed and childless within a few moments, as she stood there in her white dress, coming forth like a ghost from the chamber of the dead, the candle she held lighting up her face, and contrasting its pallor with the dark hair that fell disordered round it, its beauty radiant even through features worn with fatigue and sorrow. She was calm and even tearless, though the trembling lip told of the effort to restrain the emotion she felt. "Dear friend," she said, taking my hand, "I was coming to seek you; forgive my selfishness in neglecting you so long; but you will understand"—glancing at the door above—"how occupied I have been." "Where," I began, "is "——"my boy?" she answered, anticipating my question. "I have laid him by his father. But now your wounds must be cared for; how pale and faint you look!—rest here a moment,"—and, descending to the dining-room, she returned with some wine, which I gratefully drank, and then, making me sit down on the top step of the stairs, she brought water and linen, and, cutting off the sleeve of my coat, bathed and bandaged my

wounds. 'Twas I who felt selfish for thus adding to her
troubles; but in truth I was too weak to have much will
left, and stood in need of the help which she forced me
to accept; and the dressing of my wounds afforded indescribable relief. While thus tending me, she explained
in broken sentences how matters stood. Every room
but her own, and the little parlour into which with Wood's
help she had carried me, was full of soldiers. Wood had
been taken away to work at repairing the railroad, and
Lucy had run off from fright; but the cook had stopped
at her post, and had served up supper and opened
the cellar for the soldiers' use: she herself did not
understand what they said, and they were rough and
boorish, but not uncivil. I should now go, she said,
when my wounds were dressed, to look after my own
home, where I might be wanted; for herself, she wished
only to be allowed to remain watching there—glancing
at the room where lay the bodies of her husband and
child—where she would not be molested. I felt that
her advice was good. I could be of no use as protection,
and I had an anxious longing to know what had become
of my sick mother and sister; besides, some arrange-
ment must be made for the burial. I therefore limped
away. There was no need to express thanks on either
side, and the grief was too deep to be reached by any
outward show of sympathy.

Outside the house there was a good deal of movement and bustle; many carts going along, the wag-
goners, from Sussex and Surrey, evidently impressed and
guarded by soldiers; and although no gas was burning,
the road towards Kingston was well lighted by torches
held by persons standing at short intervals in line, who
had been seized for the duty, some of them the tenants
of neighbouring villas. Almost the first of these torch-
bearers I came to was an old gentleman whose face I was

well acquainted with, from having frequently travelled up
and down in the same train with him. He was a senior
clerk in a Government office, I believe, and was a mild-
looking old man with a prim face and a long neck, which
he used to wrap in a white double neckcloth, a thing
even in those days seldom seen. Even in that moment
of bitterness I could not help being amused by the
absurd figure this poor old fellow presented, with his
solemn face and long cravat doing penance with a torch
in front of his own gate, to light up the path of our
conquerors. But a more serious object now presented
itself, a corporal's guard passing by, with two English
volunteers in charge, their hands tied behind their backs.
They cast an imploring glance at me, and I stepped
into the road to ask the corporal what was the matter,
and even ventured, as he was passing on, to lay my
hand on his sleeve. "Auf dem Wege, Spitzbube!" cried
the brute, lifting his rifle as if to knock me down. "Must
one prisoners who fire at us let shoot," he went on to add;
and shot the poor fellows would have been, I suppose, if
I had not interceded with an officer, who happened to
be riding by. "Herr Hauptmann," I cried, as loud as I
could, "is this your discipline, to let unarmed prisoners
be shot without orders?" The officer, thus appealed to,
reined in his horse, and halted the guard till he heard
what I had to say. My knowledge of other languages
here stood me in good stead, for the prisoners, north-
country factory hands apparently, were of course utterly
unable to make themselves understood, and did not even
know in what they had offended. I therefore interpreted
their explanation : they had been left behind while skir-
mishing near Ditton, in a barn, and coming out of their
hiding-place in the midst of a party of the enemy, with
their rifles in their hands, the latter thought they were
going to fire at them from behind. It was a wonder

they were not shot down on the spot. The captain heard the tale, and then told the guard to let them go, and they slunk off at once into a by-road. He was a fine soldier-like man, but nothing could exceed the insolence of his manner, which was perhaps all the greater because it seemed not intentional, but to arise from a sense of immeasurable superiority. Between the lame *freiwilliger* pleading for his comrades, and the captain of the conquering army, there was, in his view, an infinite gulf. Had the two men been dogs, their fate could not have been decided more contemptuously. They were let go simply because they were not worth keeping as prisoners, and perhaps to kill any living thing without cause went against the *hauptmann's* sense of justice. But why speak of this insult in particular? Had not every man who lived then his tale to tell of humiliation and degradation? For it was the same story everywhere. After the first stand in line, and when once they had got us on the march, the enemy laughed at us. Our handful of regular troops was sacrificed almost to a man in a vain conflict with numbers; our volunteers and militia, with officers who did not know their work, without ammunition or equipment, or staff to superintend, starving in the midst of plenty, we had soon become a helpless mob, fighting desperately here and there, but with whom, as a manœuvring army, the disciplined invaders did just what they pleased. Happy those whose bones whitened the fields of Surrey; they at least were spared the disgrace we lived to endure. Even you, who have never known what it is to live otherwise than on sufferance, even your cheeks burn when we talk of these days; think, then, what those endured who, like your grandfather, had been citizens of the proudest nation on earth, which had never known disgrace or defeat, and whose boast it used to be that they bore a flag on which

the sun never set ! We had heard of generosity in war;
we found none : the war was made by us, it was said, ·
and we must take the consequences. London and our
only arsenal captured, we were at the mercy of our
captors, and right heavily did they tread on our necks.
Need I tell you the rest?—of the ransom we had to pay,
and the taxes raised to cover it, which keep us paupers
to this day?—the brutal frankness that announced we
must give place to a new naval Power, and be made
harmless for revenge?—the victorious troops living at
free quarters, the yoke they put on us made the more
galling that their requisitions had a semblance of method
and legality? Better have been robbed at first hand by
the soldiery themselves, than through our own magistrates made the instruments for extortion. How we lived
through the degradation we daily and hourly underwent,
I hardly even now understand. And what was there left
to us to live for? Stripped of our colonies; Canada and
the West Indies gone to America; Australia forced to
separate; India lost for ever, after the English there had
all been destroyed, vainly trying to hold the country
when cut off from aid by their countrymen; Gibraltar
and Malta ceded to the new naval Power; Ireland independent and in perpetual anarchy and revolution. When
I look at my country as it is now—its trade gone, its
factories silent, its harbours empty, a prey to pauperism
and decay—when I see all this, and think what Great
Britain was in my youth, I ask myself whether I have
really a heart or any sense of patriotism that I should
have witnessed such degradation and still care to live !
France was different. There, too, they had to eat the
bread of tribulation under the yoke of the conqueror !
their fall was hardly more sudden or violent than ours;
but war could not take away their rich soil; they had no
colonies to lose; their broad lands, which made their

wealth, remained to them; and they rose again from the blow. But our people could not be got to see how artificial our prosperity was—that it all rested on foreign trade and financial credit; that the course of trade once turned away from us, even for a time, it might never return; and that our credit once shaken might never be restored. To hear men talk in those days, you would have thought that Providence had ordained that our Government should always borrow at three per cent, and that trade came to us because we lived in a foggy little island set in a boisterous sea. They could not be got to see that the wealth heaped up on every side was not created in the country, but in India and China, and other parts of the world; and that it would be quite possible for the people who made money by buying and selling the natural treasures of the earth, to go and live in other places, and take their profits with them. Nor would men believe that there could ever be an end to our coal and iron, or that they would get to be so much dearer than the coal and iron of America that it would no longer be worth while to work them, and that therefore we ought to insure against the loss of our artificial position as the great centre of trade, by making ourselves secure and strong and respected. We thought we were living in a commercial millennium, which must last for a thousand years at least. After all, the bitterest part of our reflection is, that all this misery and decay might have been so easily prevented, and that we brought it about ourselves by our own shortsighted recklessness. There, across the narrow Straits, was the writing on the wall, but we would not choose to read it. The warnings of the few were drowned in the voice of the multitude. Power was then passing away from the class which had been used to rule, and to face political dangers, and which had brought the nation with honour unsullied through former struggles, into the hands of the lower classes, uneducated, untrained to the use of political rights, and swayed by demagogues ; and the few who were wise in their generation were denounced as alarmists, or as aristocrats who sought their own aggrandisement by wasting public money on bloated armaments. The rich were idle and luxurious ; the poor grudged the cost of defence. Politics had become a mere bidding for Radical votes, and those who should have led the nation stooped rather to pander to the selfishness of the day, and humoured the popular cry which denounced those who would secure the defence of the nation by enforced arming of its manhood, as interfering with the liberties of the people. Truly the nation was ripe for a fall ; but when I reflect how a little firmness and self-denial, or political courage and foresight, might have averted the disaster, I feel that the judgment must have really been deserved. A nation too selfish to defend its liberty, could not have been fit to retain it. To you, my grandchildren, who are now going to seek a new home in a more prosperous land, let not this bitter lesson be lost upon you in the country of your adoption. For me, I am too old to begin life again in a strange country ; and hard and evil as have been my days, it is not much to await in solitude the time which cannot now be far off, when my old bones will be laid to rest in the soil I have loved so well, and whose happiness and honour I have so long survived.

THE NAVAL & MILITARY PRESS
Specialist Books For The Serious Student Of Conflict

Military book enthusiasts now have a place on the internet dedicated to themselves. Our site is the most extensive devoted to military history on the web. You can browse and shop through our vast range of titles by time period or by theme, or use our advanced search facilities to find areas of specific interest.

The Naval & Military Press Ltd was founded in 1991 and quickly established itself as a mecca for the military enthusiast. Over 35,000 customers worldwide enjoy receiving our booklist which contains many hundreds of first-class books. With the advances in technology we are now pleased to show all of you with access to the internet our full catalogue. Updated regularly, you can count on the same level of service that our existing customers enjoy.

Our own publications feature strongly on both our list and our website. The innovative approach we have to military bookselling and our commitment to publishing have made us Britain's leading independent military bookseller.

Many titles featured on this website are not unavailable through any other source in the world.

www.naval-military-press.com

General Sir Ian Hamilton's
Staff Officer's Scrap-Book during the Russo–Japanese War 1904–1905
9781474538077

As Hamilton was the military attaché of the British Indian Army serving with the Japanese army in Manchuria during the Russo-Japanese War, he was well placed to publish in 1907 this impressive eye witness account to a military confrontation between a well-known European army and a less-familiar Asian army. Good maps (many in colour), a full index and 600+ pages make this facsimile two-volume set a fine reference for the modern scholar, of a war that is still the classic example of a conflict waged for purely imperialistic motives, a rivalry for the control of Korea and Manchuria and indeed for the mastery of the Far East and China.

The Golden Chersonese and the way thither
9781905748198

A delightful description of her travels in Malaya and China in the 1880s by that intrepid lady Isabella L. Bird, first female member of the Royal Geographical Society and doyenne of all women travel writers.

NOTES FROM A JOURNAL OF RESEARCH INTO THE NATURAL HISTORY OF THE COUNTRIES VISITED DURING THE VOYAGE OF H.M.S. SAMARANG under the command of Captain Sir Edward Belcher, C.B., F.R.A.S.
9781905748013

Like Darwin on the Beagle, surgeon Arthur Adams was a naturalist with this 1843-45 Naval expedition to Japan and the Indian and China Seas. Contains fascinating descriptions of the region's flora and fauna.

LOW`S HISTORY of the INDIAN NAVY
9781474536530

This is an extremely rare work, in its original edition, and covers the life span of the Indian Navy, 1600 to 1863. Operations from the Persian Gulf to the Burma and First China Wars, from Aden to New Zealand and the Maori Wars, and the Indian Mutiny. Survey work from the Red Sea to the China Seas.

NARRATIVE OF THE EARL OF ELGIN'S MISSION TO CHINA AND JAPAN IN THE YEARS 1857, '58, '59
9781905748051

Superbly illustrated two-volume account of Lord Elgin's expeditions to the Far East in 1857-59 which resulted in the occupation of Canton, the burning of Peking's Imperial Summer Palace; and the opening of Japan to European trade.

"CHINA JIM" Being Incidents and Adventures in the Life of an Indian Mutiny Veteran
9781845748463

An account of the author's experiences in the Indian Mutiny and the Second China War. The author acquired his nickname as a result of the immense amount of loot he acquired from the Summer Palace at Peking!

CHINESE WAR, AN ACCOUNT OF ALL THE OPERATIONS OF THE BRITISH FORCES 1842
9781843428176
Detailed account of the first Chinese 'Opium war' with Britain. With 53 fascinating illustrations.

VOYAGE OF HIS MAJESTY'S SHIP ALCESTE, to China, Corea, and the Island of Lewchew, with an account of her shipwreck
9781905748068
Rather aptly summed up by the title, this book was written by the ship's surgeon on the 'Alceste' which was charged with delivering the British Embassy of Lord Amherst to China in 1816. Passing through Rio de Janeiro, the Cape of Good Hope and Batavia en-route, they arrived in the China Sea in the summer and their first meetings with the Chinese together with some of the politics of the time are described here.

OFFICIAL ACCOUNT OF THE MILITARY OPERATIONS IN CHINA 1900-1901
9781783311156
This official account of the military operations in China at the time of the Boxer Rebellion and the siege of the Foreign Legations in Peking was originally compiled by Major Norrie, a member of the Intelligence Staff of the British Contingent, China Field Force. It was considerably revised, edited and expanded by the Intelligence Department at the War Office. It begins with the rise of the Boxer Secret Society and the outbreak of hostilities against foreigners in the northern provinces, extends to cover the operations for the relief of Foreign Legations in Peking and concludes with the peace negotiations and withdrawal of the greater part of the allied forces from China, original editions are excessively rare.

THE CRUISE OF THE PEARL WITH AN ACCOUNT OF THE OPERATIONS OF THE NAVAL BRIGADE IN INDIA
9781843428206
Drawn from the unusual diary of a naval Chaplain detailing the exploits of a scratch Naval Brigade, consisting of warship crews fighting on shore, in quelling the Indian Mutiny in 1857-58. Charming, despite the grim nature of much of the material.

THE LAST CRUISE OF THE "MAJESTIC"
George Goodchild from the log book of Petty Officer J.G. Cowie
9781474539166

Interesting personal account of the service of battleship "Majestic" in the Dardanelles arranged by Goodchild from the logbook of Petty Officer J.G. Cowie. "Majestic" was a Majestic-class pre-dreadnought battleship. In early 1915, she was dispatched to the Mediterranean for service in the Dardanelles Campaign. She participated in bombardments of Turkish forts and supported the Allied landings at Gallipoli. On 27 May 1915, she was torpedoed by the German submarine U-21 at Cape Helles, sinking with the loss of 49 men.

THE COMMISSION OF HMS TERRIBLE 1898-1902
9781843425533

Naval Brigades in South African War & China 1900. Various nominal rolls.

THE NAVAL BRIGADE IN SOUTH AFRICA DURING THE YEARS 1877-78-79
9781843429203

An account of the actions of the Naval Brigade from 'HMS Active' in South Africa's Kaffir and Zulu wars in 1877-79. Written by the Brigade's principal medical officer.

THE HISTORY OF THE BALTIC CAMPAIGN OF 1854, FROM DOCUMENTS AND OTHER MATERIALS FURNISHED BY VICE-ADMIRAL SIR C. NAPIER
9781845742126

A full history of the Crimean War's 'forgotten' sideshow in the Baltic, based on the papers of the British Commander, Admiral Napier, which exonerates him from charges of incompetence.